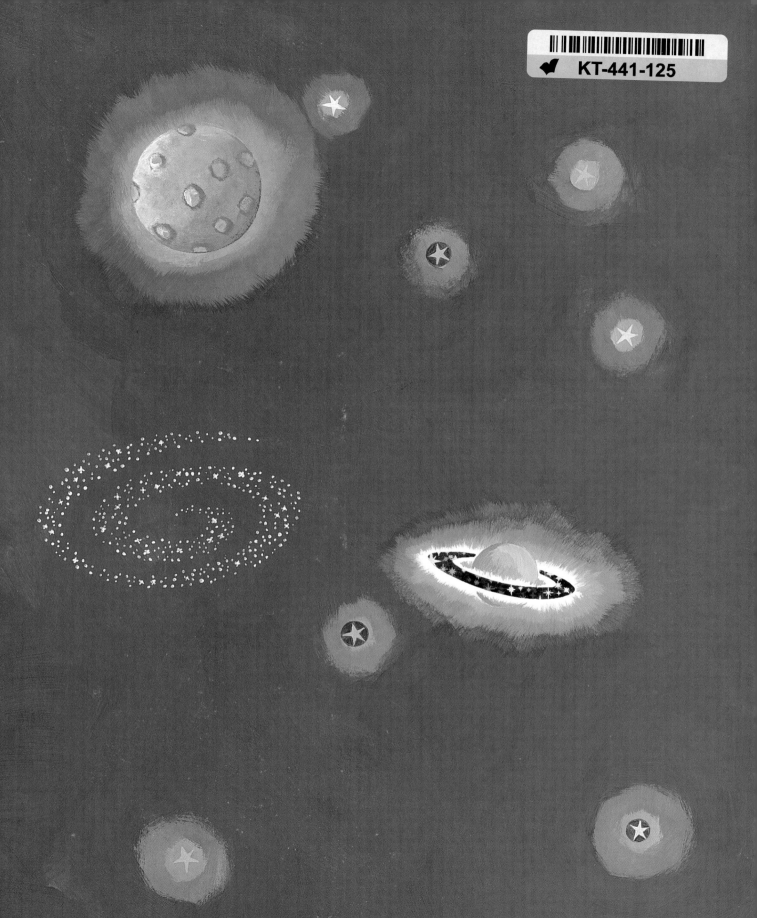

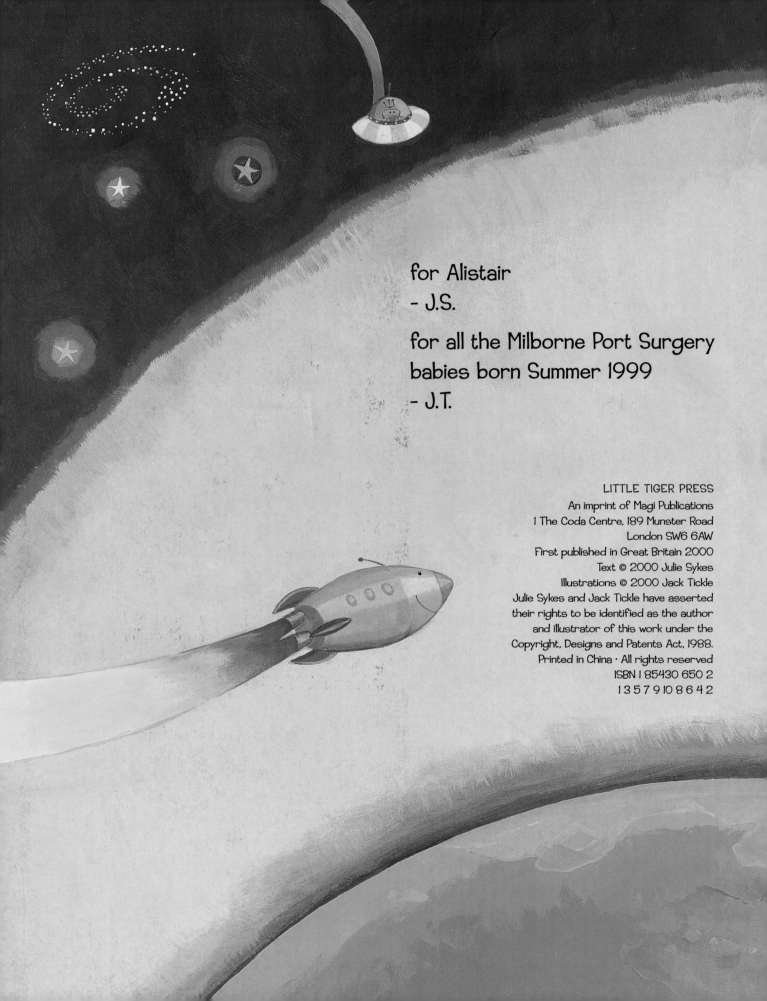

for Alistair
- J.S.

for all the Milborne Port Surgery
babies born Summer 1999
- J.T.

LITTLE TIGER PRESS
An imprint of Magi Publications
1 The Coda Centre, 189 Munster Road
London SW6 6AW
First published in Great Britain 2000
Text © 2000 Julie Sykes
Illustrations © 2000 Jack Tickle
Julie Sykes and Jack Tickle have asserted
their rights to be identified as the author
and illustrator of this work under the
Copyright, Designs and Patents Act, 1988.
Printed in China · All rights reserved
ISBN 1 85430 650 2
1 3 5 7 9 10 8 6 4 2

Little Rocket's Special Star

by Julie Sykes

Illustrated by Jack Tickle

Little Tiger Press
London

Little Rocket and her dad, Big Joe, loved looking up into space. They loved the dark sky, and the stars that sparkled high above them.

It was nearly Big Joe's birthday and Little Rocket wanted to give him something very special.

"I know," she thought. "I'll give Big Joe a shiny star all of his own."

Little Rocket waited until Big Joe was busy. Then off she set into space. Up, up, up she flew until, high above her, she could see something small and glittering.

"I've found one already," cried Little Rocket. "*There's* my star for Big Joe!" But when she got nearer...

she found it wasn't a star at all! It was Satellite Sid, circling the earth. "What are you doing so far from home?" asked Satellite Sid. "I'm looking for a star for Big Joe," said Little Rocket.

"You can't take a star from the sky,"
Satellite Sid warned her. "It will lose all
its sparkle."

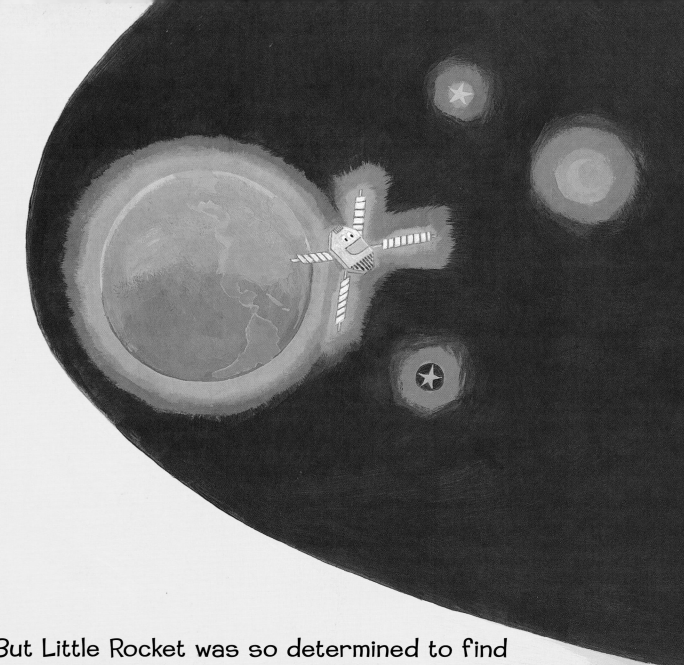

But Little Rocket was so determined to find
Big Joe a star that she didn't believe him.
"You're wrong," she cried, and off she
whizzed again.
Little Rocket flew higher and higher until,
suddenly, she saw something winking in the
darkness.
"A star!" she cried, flying quickly towards it.
Only when she got nearer...

she saw it was only the sparks
from Sammy Shuttle's engines.
"Hello, Little Rocket," called Sammy.
"Do you want a race?"
"No, I don't," said Little Rocket. "I'm
looking for a star to give to Big Joe."
"You can't take a star from the sky,"
said Sammy. "It would leave a hole."

Little Rocket thought Sammy was mistaken.
"No it wouldn't!" she cried. "There are *plenty*
of stars in the sky. No one will miss one."
And, before Sammy could argue with her, Little
Rocket zoomed on her way. She hadn't gone
far before she spotted a tiny, flickering light.
"A star!" she cried, but as she flew closer
she found . . .

it was only Andy the Astronaut's torch!
"Where are you going in such a hurry?
You nearly knocked me over!" called Andy.
"I'm searching for a star for Big Joe's
birthday," Little Rocket told him.
"You're far too small to reach the stars,"
said Andy, laughing.

"I'm *not* too small. I've flown to the moon, and the stars can't be much further," boasted Little Rocket and, with a whoosh, she flew faster and faster until she reached the moon! On its surface she could see something glimmering.
"Is that a star?" she wondered. But as Little Rocket flew nearer she found . . .

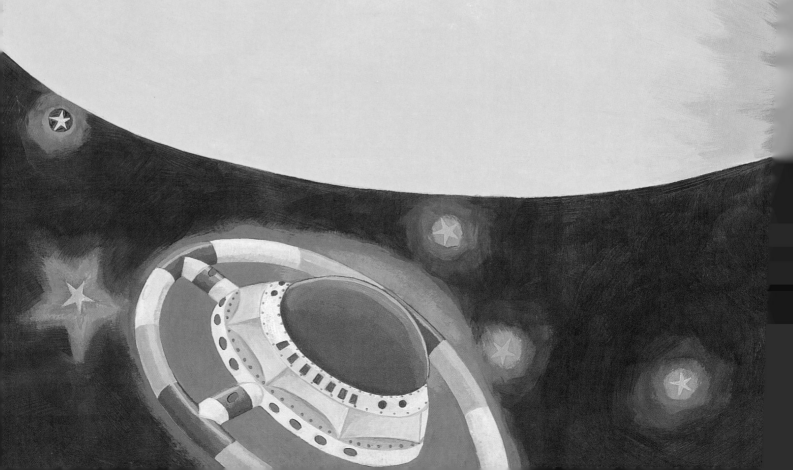

that it wasn't a star. It was
her best friend, Whizz Bang,
stuck in a crater.
"Hang on, Whizz Bang," she
called, landing beside him.
"I'll get you out."

Little Rocket tugged and she pushed and she pulled until POP! Whizz Bang slid free! "I've hurt my tail," he wailed. "I don't think I can fly." Little Rocket wanted to carry on looking for Big Joe's star, but she knew she couldn't leave poor Whizz Bang all alone.

"Don't worry, Whizz Bang. I'll help you get home safely," she said.

Whizz Bang hung on tightly
to Little Rocket's tail and
they were soon safely on
their way.

They flew past
Andy Astronaut...

and Sammy Shuttle...

and Satellite Sid...

until, at last, they landed with a bump beside
Big Joe.
"Wherever have you been?" he asked. "And
what has happened to poor Whizz Bang?"
Little Rocket told him about her search for
a special star and how she had rescued
Whizz Bang instead.
"Well done, Little Rocket. That was kind,"
said Big Joe. "But I'm glad you didn't bring
me a star. Stars are lovely, but they belong
in space where *everyone* can enjoy them.
Anyway, I already have a star."
"*You do?*" asked Little Rocket.
"Yes," said Big Joe . . .

"it's you, Little Rocket!
You are my very special
star!"

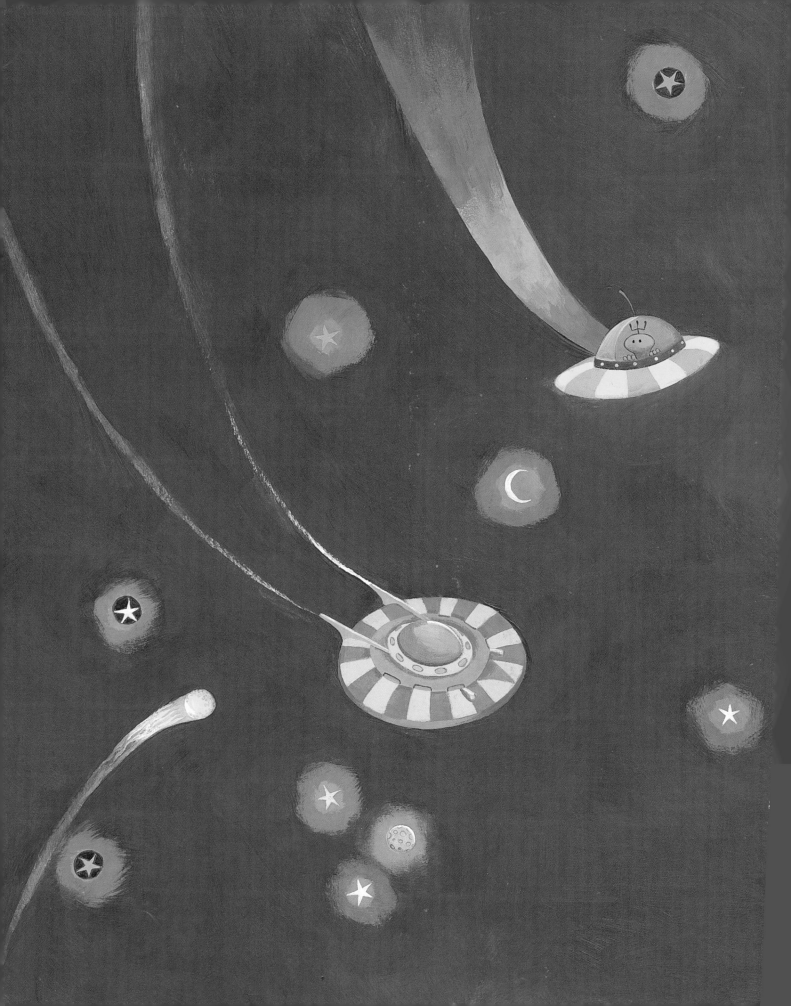